T0303735

"Daniel Riddle Rodriguez's *Low Village* maps uncharted territory. These are streets you've never seen, characters you've never met, captured in a musical vernacular bristling with energy. Rodriguez neither judges nor glamorizes the world he describes so vividly. He turns an unflinching gaze on the bonds between human beings invisible in mainstream American fiction: a boy initiating a younger friend into the life of crime, two wannabe actresses turning tricks, an addict stealing his dying grandmother's Demerol, a boy observing his alcoholic father, a girl undone at an End of the World party. This is a book like no other. Don't miss the debut of this electrifying new talent."

– Jacqueline Doyle, author of *The Missing Girl* (2017)

"Daniel Riddle Rodriguez's stories thrum with electric, dense sentences you'll stop and read again out of awe and delight. But they're not pretty for pretty's sake; they build to bursts of heartbreak as his village of desperate and downtrodden, mordant and wise, characters hustle to survive. Searing, dark, and astonishingly new, *Low Village* is ugly-pretty at its finest."

– Kara Vernor, author of
Because I Wanted to Write You a Pop Song (2016)

Low Village
Rules of the Game

Daniel Riddle Rodriguez

Nomadic Press
2016

Text copyright © 2016 by Daniel Riddle Rodriguez
Cover and spot illustrations copyright © 2016 by Arthur Johnstone and Livien Yin
Author portrait © 2016 by Arthur Johnstone

This book was made possible by a loving community of family and friends, old and new.

Requests for permission to make copies of any part of the work should be sent to
info@nomadicpress.org.

For author questions or to book a reading at your school, bookstore, or alternative
establishment, please send an email to info@nomadicpress.org.

Published by Nomadic Press, 2926 Foothill Boulevard, Oakland, California, 94601
www.nomadicpress.org

First Edition
First Printing

Printed in the United States

Library of Congress Cataloging-in-Publication Data
Rodriguez, Daniel Riddle 1983 –
Low Village: Rules of the Game / written by Daniel Riddle Rodriguez; illustrated by Arthur
Johnstone and Livien Yin
p. cm.
Summary: *Low Village* explores the symbiotic relationship between dominant and
submissive personalities: fathers and sons, hustlers and hoes, hunters and their human
prey—characters consumed by ambition and wracked with guilt.
[1. FICTION / Subjects & Themes / Relationships. 2. FICTION / Subjects & Themes /
Urban. 3. FICTION / Subjects & Themes / Addiction.] I. Title.

2016953750

ISBN: 978-0-9970933-8-4

The illustrations in this book were created using pen and marker on Canson paper.
The type was set in Garamond Premier Pro.
Printed and bound in the United States
Typesetting and book design by J. K. Fowler
Edited by Isobel O'Hare and J. K. Fowler

for my parents, Richard and Diana Rodriguez; my best friend,
Alexander Paul Rodriguez; and my twin, Katy Hake

CONTENTS

SOMETIMES POP IS INSIDE OF THE BOTTLE; SOMETIMES THE BOTTLE IS INSIDE OF POP

for Alexander

OR AT LEAST THAT'S what he says, your pop, mornings when you find him dawdle walking around the kitchen, dazzle-eyed and tart with the smell of Morgan. "I was inside the bottle this time," he'd say. Mom twists her face, slams their bedroom door.

Pop becomes a different man when he gets inside the bottle. He disappears himself. A little scotch and soda water, he's a brand new guy. Mom is on to his act, though, says it's not that new. "You can see for yourself," she says. "God, I know I gave you eyes."

The new guy is taller than Pop (you can see for yourself). He wears cotton tank tops and flexes his arms when he talks. He's a smoker, too, and hours after he's left the living room you can still smell the air of him. The way a spent match takes over your coat pocket, some stale thing that settles into the fibers. "And look at how he eats," Mom says, pointing with her fork across the table. The new guy chomping pizza, cheese looping from his mouth, thick and white as spit on a bulldog. "He's a problem," she says, stabbing her plate. "A big one."

It used to be Pop worked a dry week and only brought out the new guy on off-days. Sundays mostly. It worked like this: Pop got inside of the bottle and New Guy got out. He used to jump up and down, pumping his fists whenever the Raiders took the over. New Guy yelled at the screen, cursed refs. "Fucking Magoos, all of them," he'd say. When they scored, he did a little Juba dance in the living room before spiking the remote, sending broken pieces of plastic everywhere. Mom would slam their door, then, same as she does now, but gently, gently. Soft because she knew, come morning, Pop would be on his hands and knees, picking plastic out the carpet fibers, a white-flag look on his face and *eye-owe-you* in his mouth. This was when he was still working the Frito-Lay factory at the foot of Grant Avenue. Back then he'd stuff Hefty bags full of potato chips and shoulder the goods like a velvet sack, and you'd get fat on chips till the salt split your tongue. Then all of a sudden he's laid off and spending more and more time climbing into the bottle, practicing his magic trick. The only chips he shoulders these days are proverbial.

This is what you know: New Guy speaks in *quids* and *pro quos* but does not like ultimatums. You know this because he says so. All the time. He says so in church when he skips the wafer line to abuse the Eucharist cup, streaks of burgundy in his beard. He says so at the supermarket, full basket in the checkout line and the card ain't cutting it. "Run it again," New Guy tells the clerk, winking at her like God didn't give Mom eyes. "Third time's the charm, right?" And when Mom drops a stack of bills onto his lap like an anvil, her face all *what the fuck*, New Guy is out the door without a word—a skinny, sweaty man, shadow getting long.

Sometimes Pop defends the new guy. He tries to play at devil's advocate. "Let go and let God," he tells us. "I mean, it *is* what it *is*, right?" And then he goes on about the new guy isn't so bad, after all; how if you only knew what it was like *being* a new guy; how difficult it is to catch a break with those wrists of his, thin as they are; to shoulder the world with arms so small. "Cut the guy some slack," Pop says. "Atlas gotta shrug sometime, right?"

New Guy shrugged off another job search today so he could stand in the doorway and pick paint chips off the lintel, drop them onto the kitchen floor. Mom is at the stove, putting matchsticks to the pilot light. Sauntering up, New Guy palms her bathrobe pockets from behind, pulling her into his crotch and holding her there till she squirms free. "I've got the gas on," Mom says in a voice like she means it this time—a snapped string on a guitar. "You want to blow us up?" She cocks her arm and throws the box of matches at New Guy, hitting him square in the mouth. And then it's like everything in the kitchen stops to see what he's going to do, except he isn't doing anything but staring at the floor as if he's counting up the matches. Mom cocks her head like she wants something from him that he doesn't have. And now, seeing he doesn't have it, she walks out the room, leaving New Guy behind. Alone. Standing there like some lone General surveying land shelled to rubble on his order, and what he surveyed he didn't like. For a moment you can see Pop again, a flash in the face, some gathered force quaking in the eyebrows. Behind the eyes, a man tied to a chair, gagged stupid and bleeding. He opens the freezer door, snags a bottle from the icebox—brown liquor, swashbuckler on the label—and brings it to his lips.

"Abracadabra," Pop says, disappearing.

RATS, TRICKS, LEGUMES

for Robert Silva

POP HATES THE SCABS, says they wouldn't know a good thing if it slapped them with a sack of pussy.

"Right in their cock-smoking faces," says Pop.

It's picket season and Pop is flying the giant rat. I ride shotgun to work the pump, keep coffee for the cowboys.

"It's just the ignorance," Jim says. Jim is one of the cowboys. He sidearms Johnny Walker but knows how to pitch a wrench.

"No shit," says Pop. "It's thanks to us they have a weekend."

"I thought that was 'cause of Jesus," I say.

"Jackshit Jesus," Pop says. "He's still a scab carpenter, savior or no."

Jim looks wistful, says, "If they only knew."

"Just work the pump," says Pop. "We gotta beat the pour."

The two-gate system nipped balls from the picket line. Union busters make it so open shops can cross gate two while trade guys mill around gate one, shredding paper signs and frothing on their steel-toes. Most scabs sling Spanish curses through the chain-link; the brave ones sling food; the really brave ones don't miss. The cowboys here riddled with *putos* and cobbed corn.

But on pour day we get our balls back.

We put pressure to the polyvinyl rat until his eyes bulge thirty feet high, and the white collars cup their eyes against their office windows, face the whiskers. Sometimes the boys fit him with a bandana—old bed sheets daisy-chained and dyed red—to hearken the beast days when life was cheaper and sidearms were literal. When the cock smokers got hit with worse things than muff.

"The good old days," Jim says.

I nod but keep cutting foam and casting glances at Pop, who's swilling scotch now, too, and flinging cigarette butts to the gutter, whipping the meeker boys—apprentices and newly vested journeymen—into bravehearts.

"What do we want?" he says. "When do we want it?"

The foam is for the cheese. The cheese is Pop's brainchild. He has one every strike. He wakes me up with a boot to the box spring and *Eureka!* on his lips. He used to wake Mom this way 'til she decided to do her waking elsewhere, left him a Dear John, said it was she not he. But when I'm scrubbing sheets free of tread stains or carving cheese wheels for a rubber rodent, I'm pretty sure it's he.

"Scabby needs a prop," Pop said. "Get up and make a Jarlsberg."

Boot. Box spring. Eureka!

15

Robert says Jarlsberg is Swiss cheese made by Norwegians. Robert is Jim's son. He rides shotgun, too, but doesn't give a fuck about a bunch of shitkickers. "You have no idea how many fucks I don't give," Robert would say. Our dads are like brothers because they've been threading steel and perambulating drunk from the same pubs for two decades. They are shareholders of an ethos: the world's a feudal system; if you're not vested then you carry tools and your chin is made for scraping. Robert and I are brothers because our chins match scrape for scrape. Plus we have no mothers. His didn't bother with a Dear Anybody, just one day up and vanished.

"It's not that I miss her," he said once. "She left before I could even barely read."

I told him he could barely read still—just to fill the silence.

"Read this," he said, giving me the finger.

So these days I let Robert fill the silence. That's the *quid*. The *pro quo*, he helps with the cheese.

"I'll make some holes," he says, burning the foam with his cigarette. "The Teamsters are going to shit," he says. "They love weekends and hate scabs like your pop does."

Me, I don't hate the scabs. I can see both sides of a thing. Mr. Morris, my guidance counselor, said it's a sign of intelligence. Sitting in a dimpled-leather rolling chair, wearing an Einstein tee shirt, he stabbed blueberries with an oyster fork and narrowed down the future.

"So you're saying I'm intelligent," I said.

"There are open doors," he said.

"Limitless horizon."

"Not that many doors."

All seniors take it, this door-closing test. Passed around during free period, the blackened bubbles are read by a computer that decides tomorrow: *Congratulations, Mr. So-and-so. Of the world's many things, you are suited for, like, three.*

"Someone has to drive the bus," Mr. Morris would say. "A lucky few get to own it." He looked at me then lanced a wayward berry. "No, not that lucky."

My computer said option one: philosopher.

"I didn't know option ones still existed."

"They're certainly an endangered species," Morris said. "But option two requires a special drivers license."

"Who the fuck is Mr. Morris?" Jim says now. "Tell him my paycheck could cut his check a check."

Jim's a dying breed of option one.

"How does that work exactly?" I say. "I mean, who does the signing? Or the cashing even?"

"This does," Jim says, gives me the finger. "You got it?"

"Got it," I say.

Outside the picket line, a migrant woman with a pushcart offers mango and the chance to pay for it—a straw basket, a shallow pool of copper and grubby ones, but I know she keeps cash in a nest of adipose tissue due south. She knows I know it, makes a face she brought from home, a country still in its beast days. *Don't try me*, it says.

"I'll only try the mango," I say.

She pares the skin and carves at the fruit like a bonsai tree, tops it with lemon and chili powder. She pumps quarters from her waist and wants to know why a rat?

The rubber rat banks back and forth with the breeze, its handkerchief a large red windsock.

"Because they're ignorant," I say.

"Oh no," she says. "*Ratas* are *deber*. You take my words for it."

If you take her words for it, Pushcart will tell you she kept them as pets. The *ratas*. As a kid. Taught them peanut tricks: shell-shucking, peanut butter from a spoon, the palm.

"That is *deber*," I say.

"What's clever?" says Robert.

"Rats, tricks, legumes."

"What about cheese?"

"No," Pushcart says. "They *donnat* eat the *sheeze*."

"Take her words for it," I say.

"What about her mangoes?" Robert says, pantomimes a handful of chestfruit.

She's back on the quarter pump.

Paring knife, lemon, chili.

Bonsai.

Pop remembers Jim's good days. They joined the UA in the same year, when unionism was synonymous with lion's share and selective hiring kept the lions white. Training was hands-on, the slow-moving apprentice a target for screwed elbows and threaded nipples. It's how Jim learned to pitch his wrench, put enough English on it to unhat an apprentice without turning his lights all the way out. The good old boys are all the same: an entire generation of blue-collared cowboys, men who pass rough hands over their progeny.

Robert has rough hands so he drew a penis on his Scantron, a few darkened bubbles for seminal fluid. Mr. Morris says our friendship has a shelf life. Robert's doors lead to places where they'll stuff a swab in his mouth, smear ink on his fingers. Places where they take your shoelaces just in case. "He's looking for an alibi," Mr. Morris said. " A corroborating witness. Someone to lie with a hand on King James."

If Robert had fucks to give he'd probably be a Morris, too. "Only to subvert the system," he'd say. "All those little minds molded in my image. Can't you imagine?"

I say I can't even though I can. *So help me God*, the little minds say.

But since he's fuck-deficient, Robert spends most days trying to subvert the future. I'm playing at his alibi—at least until our expiration date.

Now the cheese is finished. Scabby the Rat holds it to his chest and waits for the cement truck rumble.

Pop wants to know what's taking them so fucking long.

"What's taking them so fucking long?" he says.

Teamsters are tough, not crazy tough like the beam-walkers, or leather boot tough like the laborers—back-breakers with brine-soaked skin—but they maintain their strength in numbers. And they never cross a picket line. The union busters add a second gate; we stand in front of it and the Teamsters park their rigs and let the concrete churn until the general contractor says *Uncle*. They always do, usually before the dirt cakes the mud flaps.

Pop is relying on Teamster muscle, that trouser swell of balls.

He's down to a tank top now. Jim beside him, a lit cigarette dangling. They've got their faces to the gate, eyes framed by the links. "Okay, José," says Pop. "I see you, you little rat." The rats stare back, flexing their wifebeater tans and spitting between their boots. Everybody hating everybody, and everybody pissing in the dirt trying to spot-measure the distance.

All I do is pray for rain.

Or a stiff wind, blow the piss back at them.

One of the meek hooks me at the elbow. "You're the big man's son," he says, pointing to Pop. "So what's he really like?"

I shrug. "Mostly like this."

I spend a lot of mornings working on brainchildren, skipping class—doubling down on option two, adding color to my collar. Robert skips too but bones up his reading. We sit around the bedroom cracking schoolbook spines. Robert likes to break the backs.

"Who're you going to read to when I'm not around?" I said once.

"I don't even know what that means," he said. "Besides, when are you not around?"

"Fuck off," I said. "I've got doors. Horizons."

"I like the hardbacks best," he said, dislocating one.

Later he brought other books, read aloud the stuff that wasn't assigned in school. *Did you know that tuberculosis ravaged the cradle of civilization, like, four thousand years ago? he said. The Egyptians and Greeks, their children, all manner of Fertile Crescent critter wiped out. Then there was the plague, the black one, one in three pockets posied. Have you seen what an Agent Orange baby looks like?*

"Look," he said then. "I brought pictures."

All those inflated skulls and pop-out peepers I can't unsee.

"Those were somebody's good old days," I said, trying to blink away plague.

"Not his," Robert said, flashing Viet Cong critter.

Those Bette Davis eyes.

Other philosophers take note: the weekend thing, it really was Jesus, or at least his followers, disciples of disciples—the blue-collared sons of Abraham wanting to keep holy the holy day. Then it was Orthodox Jews observing Shabbos. We get hammered on Rolling Rock and lip gristle from ribs because our savior—in his wisdom—makes allowances. Thank him even if the jackshit hammered cogs without a collective bargaining agreement.

"He's also a statutory rapist," Robert says now, sitting on the curb like a dustbowl farmer, dirty in his overalls. "The world's first registered sex offender," he says. "I won't even mention the whole sex-with-the-mom thing."

"At least he had a mom," I say.

"Touché," Robert says, chomps mango and spits.

The picket line is thick with drink. The boys have ditched the bullhorns for hand tools. Pop handed them out. Jim showed them how to brandish.

Pop looks like Patton in Carhartt work pants. He hands each of the cowboys a wrench: monkey wrench, pipe wrench, hammer wrench, all the wrenches. He says to them, "Ask not what your union can do for you . . ."

The general contractor cancelled the pour. Rescheduled it really. Sometime between the second gate and the Jarlsberg, the clever rat made the picket line obsolete. Now he wants to negotiate with a scattershot gaggle of disgraced cowhands, drunk, looking to nip the horn. He comes out the trailer, hat in hand, with an olive-branch look on his face. Another peanut trick.

"Unless you're coming to tell me you're shit-canning the *vatos*, you're wasting your fucking time," says Pop.

The general's wasting his fucking time. There actually seems to be more *vatos*, a multitude of *vatos*, a *vato* plethora scheming on our flank. I scan the crowd, wondering which one of them is their Pop. Their Jim and Robert.

Which one of them pours the coffee?

Insults are exchanged, allusions to butt-fucking, throat-fucking, fist-fucking, the entire fucking spectrum. The general promises to return with the law, that he'll have you assholes in cages. I try to visualize the threat: a drunk tank full of good old boys blowing shit over a phone call, their confiscated shoelaces. The assholes boo, belt him with soda cans that crack their heads on the shale and spin. Some of them roar and drag their wrenches across the fence like prison cups.

"Finally," Robert says, "some action. Looks like we won't have a choice."

"How about inaction," I say.

"As a choice?"

"Yeah."

"That sounds a lot like faggotry," says Robert. "Or a lot like Mr. Morris. Probably both."

"Fuck off," I say. "Read this."

Pop waves me over, tucks me into his armpit. "Have a bit to cure what ails you," he says, giving me the Johnny Walker.

"I'm not ailing," I say, taking it

"It'll put hair on your chest," he says. "Your balls, too."

"We don't have any balls."

"Just give it a minute."

It may be the alcohol or whatever, but the cowboys are hugging.

Slapping each other on the ass like we just took the pennant.

Pop takes me by the chin. "Why didn't you throw anything?"

"Like what?"

"Like anything."

"He's not even a scab, Pop."

"He hired them."

"They're cheap help," I say.

"Birds of a feather."

"Nobody wants to trowel pavement, Pop."

"He made his bed."

"What?"

"He has to lay down sometime." Pop gestures like that time is now. "Do the right thing here and help tip the gate. From the bottom up. No, not like that, jackshit. Like this…"

Robert and I stand together and watch them tip the gate. The scabs on the other side tipping back. Everybody still hating everybody.

"This is like one big rumble in a movie about rumbling," says Robert.

One of the cowboys catches a finishing trowel to the forehead and goes down. His apprentice falls with him. The cowboys return with a volley of monkey wrenches. The gate finally gives and everyone spills over.

When people really fight, it can look a lot like fucking if you stand back far enough, with all the grunting and pulling and the mishmash of blooming flesh, the tears.

Robert and I aren't that far back so it looks a lot like rape.

"I think this is it," I say.

"What's it?"

"I think I'm done with this."

"The fight?"

"Striking, pickets, the union. Cheese."

"You're on strike from striking?"

"Indefinitely."

"Boycotting the boycott."

"Yeah."

"What about your pop?" Robert says.

"I think I'm boycotting him, too."

"Are you going to your Mom's?"

I look at the dog pile of tradesmen and scabs. I see Jim surfing the pile, wrench in hand, trying to bring back the asbestos days.

Pop looks at me, says, "We're winning!"

"Are you going to finish school?" Robert says.

The general has a pile driver pinned beneath the bulk of him, one of the soda throwers. "Take this, you fuck," he screams.

I say, "I'm going to look for fewer options."

"Fewer than two?"

I show him my hands, make claws. "These are endangered," I say.

"I'm not sure what that even means," Robert says.

"It means I'm crossing that picket."

I pick up a battered hard hat from the dirt, fix it on my head. I walk toward all the scabs and sparkies and wharfies, the tin-knockers and turd-herders, the men who put wrenches to steel and use bare flesh to hold back, toward that pile of wifeless November nobodies.

I picture my mother watching me from wherever it is she watches things, maybe with the white-collars, her hands cupping glass, making fog with her nostrils. Maybe Robert's mom is with her. I'll show them the way to fix a thing is to walk towards it. Show them the other side.

Robert should walk with me. You don't need too many fucks to subvert the system, be a philosopher too. I can loan him a few.

I turn around to tell him this, but the cruisers are already pulling up, blue and reds flashing, bullhorn feedback. Guns.

"All right, you assholes. Freeze."

The assholes do.

SHORTLY AFTER HER FIRST period, Valentine begins finding traps around her house. At first they are small—snares made of shoelace that snake along the hallway, glue traps in her bedroom closet—and sporadic. In no time, though, she's finding larger traps: nets that span the length of her driveway, fishing lures cast from panel vans, muscle cars, matte-black Mustangs measled with Bondo.

Her mother blames it on the boys, says they turn into hunters whenever girls are around. "But don't take my word for it," she says. "You can see for yourself."

She sees her friends disappearing. They follow breadcrumbs into dark station wagons. Fall into wolf pits outside their bedroom windows. Bite hooks and vanish. Men move shade-like through the neighborhood, while mothers, diva-eyed and desperate, burn candles. Faces on milk cartons resemble her own. Her street is dense with tree-blinds.

Valentine spends most of her days springing bear traps with sticks. The creek bed behind her house is littered with them. She used to lose whole summers here, count down hours in an algebra lost upon her mother, squat with the boys, trap lizards and crush crawdads with rocks. What happened to those boys? They look so much like their fathers now, with their foxtail caps and teeth, their frothy mouths impossibly large. Where did they go? They have left and become the patron saints of somewhere else. They are brake dust, diesel fumes. They are smoke. She sings their names into the mouth of the creek's underpass, calls the echo gospel.

She wants to believe they'll come back, searching for pieces they left behind. The way her mother will eventually lose herself, brain scattered like marbles across the floor, and spend the rest of her nights searching. A flashlight white-knuckled in her hand, the dark edges of herself getting darker.

In history class, a man stares down her blouse and tells her the brush fire is the land's biography. They put entire forests to flame to attract big game, killed them in droves while they grazed. At her prom, a boy leans into her ear, whispers, "There is a soft spot between a rock and a hard place, and I know exactly where it is, I can prove it." And even though she knows exactly where "exactly" is, she lets him prove it anyway. He sinks teeth into her neck, fills her mouth with the saltlick of his fingers. This is how she knows she'll be recognized: by the smell of her scorched-earth hair, the sulfur on her breath.

She wants to believe that no one can crave what truly harms them. That her body is more than a threshold for smash and grab, break and enter. The tongue more than a tool for soft power, a whip, a bitch-be-cool stick to bludgeon you grateful.

In a hospital room, she sits at the foot of the bed. Starched white sheets, flowers. The small woman in the bed getting smaller, shrinking into something that will fit inside an upturned palm, the hollow belly of a spoon, a collapsing vein. "Someday this war is going to end," her mother says, in a voice that is both her own and not. The way a tree is both the house you build and the box that buries you. Outside, everything is meat, hide-and-tallow trade, things to be won in a war. Outside, the world is a sawmill that swallows you whole, spits you out. And why not make the best of bad between the binge and purge?

There's an end to you and it looks like this: You wake up in a stranger's bed. You wake up, a coil-spring trap on your leg, key in his hand. You wake up, put your paw between your teeth. Bite down.

ANOTHER NIGHT AT JOHN'S, another game of ring around the nostril. The coke was dope, fishscale phylum, and they were on their third gram. John handled things—the mirror, the asbestos white cocaine—and carved powder rails large enough to cast shadows on the glass. He saw things. Blinking lights that danced on the ceiling.

Rule number one: Stop Using When You Start Seeing Things.
John was breaking rules again.
Kelly and his girlfriend, January, were on the couch in John's basement. Their faces were numb. They scraped gums. Kelly's tongue a bucket brigade pouring flora and fauna into her throat.
John, armed with a straw, chased the asbestos away.
The lights on the ceiling blinked until they didn't.
The couch in John's basement was really his mother's couch because it was really his mother's basement; John just sometimes paid the rent, the cable bill, but mostly he squatted with Kelly and hatched get-rich-slow schemes.
Like now.
"So we'll be doormen, then?" John said.
"No, not really, dude," Kelly said, taking the mirror into his lap. "Think bigger."
"Security?"
"Bigger, dude."
John was confused so he said, "I'm confused."
January wiped her nose across her arm. "It's simple," she said. "The Berlin Wall needs guys, not bouncers really, screeners. Go-betweens. Rules say it's hands-off but girls date anyway. You guys make sure everything goes right."
"So … we'll be like pimps, then?" John said.
"Not really," said Kelly. "More like middlemen."
"No," January said. "John's right. More like pimps."

Rule number two: Stop Using When Your Nose Bleeds.
John breaks that rule whenever he can afford to.
He can afford to tonight because he'd already jumped the postman, filched his mother's check, doubled down on a deviated septum. Bills were due the fifteenth and social security came on the first. He spent the meantime trying to make the latter meet the former.
The latter hardly cooperated.

It was a hard fight, but Kelly leased him some muscle. Besides squatting and hatching and coating his sniffles with powder, Kelly was good at other things: ambushing mail carriers and keeping close proximity to money. It was a gift. Like serendipity but with aforethought. The malicious kind.

Kelly was also good at having a bank account.

"That your mother's check?" he'd asked then. "Sign it over to me and you'll see at least double in a week."

This is how plans are hatched.

"Double?" said John.

"In a week," Kelly said. "Trust me."

If you choose to trust Kelly you'll find the way to double your money is to spend it all first. The trick is to buy enough for a deal but not so much you sit on the onion. Money isn't the only thing with a short shelf life. Kelly was full of little wisdoms. *Did you know they're paying more than triple the price in at least three states between the west and the mid?* he'd say. Or, *we can stay here, cut this with baby laxative, get a motel room in the city and really make a killing.* Or, *we can troll the Greyhound, poach a few souls willing to peddle themselves for a bump.*

"Listen John," Kelly said now. "If you don't get high on your own supply, how in the hell are you supposed to get high? Sniff once and inspire that entrepreneurial spirit."

John origamied Andrew Jackson cylindrical, said, "Baby laxative? Soul poaching? People still go for that?"

"People still go for everything. The bait and switch. The pig in a poke."

"Guys selling TV boxes full of bricks taped to the bottom ..." January offered.

"Exactly," said Kelly. "A fool and his money soon part and all that. All you gotta do is keep their gaze. Never flinch, dude, and the possibilities are endless."

Kelly told John of all things possible and endless as he popcorned the brick with a hanger, gorging on blow until rule number two came pouring out of John's nose in globs and greebles, bloody horns that painted his face a Gaucho mustache.

"Dude," said Kelly. "You're getting red on Jackson."

The former President, a cylinder no more, just a bill, blood smeared and curling.

John tried to wipe it clean. "My mom's going to kill me," he said.

"Jeez, dude," said Kelly. "All I have are these crummy singles."

Rule number three: Never Use Crummy Singles.

No one follows rule number three. Get them high enough people fucking lick George Washington's face, his chalky hairline.

Or get them drunk enough, people try to fuck you with them.

John and Kelly know this because January said so. Sitting on the couch, she said, "And you can just tell some guys iron their ones because they smell like starch. The ones, I mean. Ironed flat but still grimy—give your pussy a paper-cut on purpose."

January says all tricks are sadistic, right on down the line. Like all deadbeats speak the same language. She said, "That's where you two come in."

"Yeah, dude," said Kelly. "The girls need us to translate."

"Translate?"

"Uh-huh," said Kelly, winking, "Tell me: how's your German?"

The Berlin Wall was built some time after the original was razed. Rumor spread like a whispersong that the owner was an old Eastern Bloc national, and the bar a hat tip to the Iron Curtain, but January said the old man's only nation was "Jew." The hat a black kippah.

"The first thing you'll notice is the smell," January said. "Like body sweat and baby powder. The way bum niggas hot-press dirty jeans, spray cologne instead of bathing. But it isn't 'til you reach the private rooms that it all turns antiseptic. A coat on every surface. Like, if these walls could breathe, they'd burp bleach."

January said most tricks don't notice cuz they've got twat on the brain. She said it just like that: twat.

She said, "That is where you'll be most nights, between the stage and the back rooms. All you have to do is stand guard."

There was a large Hawaiian man whose job may not have been anything more than being large and Hawaiian. His name was Rock. All the girls said he was a teddy bear; his tattoos said he'd rather die than be dishonored.

"But you don't have to trip on him," January said. "He only covers the door, the bar."

John's post would be the no-man's land between the baby powder and the ammonia. Screening for potential sodomites and papercutters.

Something like a pimp.

If San Lorenzo houses had foyers, John would've been standing in one.

The consolation prize a cubic yard of tile—real marble, faux luxury for the rent control demographic. The air was dense, tart with the copper coin smell of his mother and TV dinners. She was in the living room, stabbing chicken fried steak with an oyster fork, watching TV.

This time it wasn't *M*A*S*H**.

Tonight was courtroom drama, a police procedural: cigarette smoke in the interrogation room, good cop/bad cop. John sat next to his mother, fingered the lace doilies and worked the remote. She coughed pieces of herself onto the floor while he explained to her the nuances:

"He's the one who did it, Ma."

John dissolved pieces of black tar in a Visine bottle, sniffed deeply to keep from nose-diving into the carpet fibers, squeezing her hand to maintain spatial orientation.

The detective played the hambone card, the perp wilting under the combination of palm strikes and police jargon:

Where you'd hide the body, pervo?

Nights like these he'd squeeze her hand and say, "It was him, Ma."

But mostly it was *M*A*S*H**.

Hunnicutt and Hawkeye.

Witty repartee.

John changed the channel.

"You were named after him," his mother said, spitting flecks of food past her dentures.

"Hawkeye?"

"John Kennedy," she said.

"That's Alan Alda, Ma."

"It was right after he died, remember? And the flags flew half-mast?"

"I was born in '78, Ma."

"But your father didn't have a flag so he named you after him."

"He never said nothin."

"After Kennedy," she said.

Ma probed the insides of her cheeks, tongued the crest of her lips, searching for disintegrated crumbs. "He had high hopes for you."

John said his father said nothing and it was true. He came from a generation that spoke mostly with their hands and wore blue collars like millstones—yoked masons and silent rebar twisters.

A working class hero.

Sodium of God's strata.

"I said your father said he had high hopes for you," she said.

"Could've been President," said John.

"Not that high," she said.

On the TV, two surgeons traded barbs back and forth—lunge, riposte, repeat—while a dress with some sort of man inside sashayed around the room.

"Looks like some work's coming up, though, Ma," John said. "A respectable place, too. Liquor license."

Ma stared miles into the screen. "Look who's hoping now," she said.

John does not remember rule four, but it should be: Don't Trust Kelly With Ma's Money.

A week after they should have seen at least double the money back, John and Kelly were standing in the living room, staring at snow.

"So, what happened?" said John.

"I think it's called white noise," said Kelly.

"I meant the money."

"Oh, that. Crazy, dude. First I grossly miscalculated supply and demand for stepped on blow in our beloved Bible Belt. Stepped too hard, we did. Plus my mule got arrested."

"No way."

"I am mule-less."

"That is totally fucked."

"She was on her way back. It was kinda random apparently, a totally unrelated incident—"

"My mom's going to kill me."

"—except they found the money on her."

"Fucked."

"So in a way I guess it does relate."

"What happens now?"

"To her? Nothing, probably. A court date, juvenile probation maybe."

"The money."

Kelly clicked the remote, surfed static. "You need to pay the bill," he said.

They stared at the TV screen, the army of black ants marching.

"At least we have January," John said. "At least we have some work."

"*Au contraire, mon frère*," said Kelly. "I have January. You have an interview." Kelly looked at a watch John hadn't noticed before. "In T-minus ninety minutes. So, you know, look sharp or whatever."

John looked himself over: Fruit of the Loom wifebeater and a pair of denim jeans that sprouted from the loom, Pro Keds. "How do I look?"

"Like a shoe-in," Kelly said, clicked the remote.

Rule number five: Don't Tell Them You're Here For The Pimp Job.

Before he broke rule five John went to the Berlin, dressed in a Polo shirt and khakis borrowed from his father's closet, his blue-collar formal wear. He stood outside the club and checked his reflection in the tinted windows. The shirt had an embroidered reptile. The khakis cuffed under the rubber soles of his Keds. There was a sign above the door that said "The Berlin Wall" and a German Shepherd leashed to a truck tire, sleeping.

John looked at its ragged ears, the button of callous on its nose. He reached into his pocket and then dumped a pinch of powder onto the meat of his fist, sniffed it. He addressed the dog.

"Here goes everything," he said, projecting indifference.

The sleeping dog snorted once, projecting the same.

Inside the club the shift was changing. New dancers. A man in a grey shirt and a pompadour shoved a mop around while the old guard—journeymen dancers grinding the rent—spent the last part of their shift with the alkies, trying to fleece them for singles, maybe a shot of Beam for the cab ride home. The DJ stacked his records. Rock was behind the bar doing barman things: polishing glasses, toweling top. He pointed a martini glass at John and said, "You're here."

"Yes, I am," said John.

"You're early."

"Showing initiative."

Rock slapped the towel over his shoulder and placed a rotary phone onto the bar top, hunched over it like he was calling the Kremlin. The phone was all red bulbs, no numbers, the center of the dial like an all white eyeball.

The Kremlin answered.

"Man says he'll see you in a minute. Just wait here by the bar."

One of the dancers, an old guardian in leopard print, saddled a barstool next to John's, fingered his collar. "I love your shirt," she said. "Crocodiles are, like, my second favorite reptile."

Before John could ask about her first, a voice said he's not a barfly.

"He's not a barfly," said the voice. "So you might as well give it up."

January, a cigarette dangling from her lip, shooed the leopard away and, leaning in, gave John one of those one-armed hugs where tits kiss the chin. "You got a light?" she said.

She was wearing a dye job and china bangs, body glitter and pasties, cat ears.

Because everyone likes pussy, she told me, just like that.

"You ever wear those for Kelly?"

"Used to," January said. "Not lately. Withdrawals, I guess. It's been, like, whiskey dick but without the whiskey."

"Crazy."

"No dick, either."

"Is there anything I can do?" John said. "I was named after a President, you know."

"Yeah, which one?"

"I don't know. The dead one. "

"My favorite." January tossed her cigarette into a beer stein, prompted a hiss of smoke. "I'm up next."

John worked his elbows on the bar top. The DJ worked the ones and twos, the wobble bass.

The striptease is an awkward waltz, but tricks don't notice cuz twat's still on the brain. For most girls the pole is more prop than dance partner, something to grab while you fling your box at the crowd, shake stretch marks invisible. Even experienced girls are graceless, in any other context an oddity—think back-bend contortion or Cirque de Soleil without the esteem—an oiled down and sparkling hood ornament. But January was a star, a constellation even. She got on stage and spread her singularity, breathed life into shitty metaphors. On the brass pole, she made dubstep feel like Mozart.

John wondered how long it would last. How long before the lambskin pops and she's squatting an eight-pound hatchling? How long before she's just another quivering mass of black leggings and swollen ankles stuffed into pink Crocs, a stoop mom smoking Newports to the filter, yelling at the back of her son's head? Will the son look like Kelly? What color would that be—tan? Is mixed a color? John remembered when flesh came in the Crayola box; remembered, too, that it was a damned close match.

He took a powder bump for nostalgia's sake.

January spun back up the pole, her redbone legs like chopper blades. "It's like she has an extra hand down there." He wondered what her flesh tone was.

"You keep those dick beaters in your pockets," Rock said, pointing to John's dick beaters. "Come on. The man will see you now."

The man had an office upstairs with one-way glass that oversaw the club, and a bank of closed-circuit televisions that assisted the overseeing. The man was old, reed-stalk thin, his face all bone and sharp angles, skin like cracked porcelain. "Can I offer you something to drink?" he said. "Water? J&B? Rock, get...I'm sorry, I didn't get your name."

"John, sir. Like the President ..."

"Right. Rock, get John here a J&B." The old man smiled. He looked like something carried by the neck, a patchwork of wrinkles stitched to the ears. He sat behind a desk too large for the room, for himself, probably for the world. An oak desk with nothing on it but the old man and a steel nameplate that read: Obadiah.

The old man smoked electronic cigarettes that blinked red when he inhaled and produced vapor instead of smoke. "I'm trying to cut back, you see. Doctor says four packs a day is four packs too many. Had a cancer scare a while back, turned out to be nothing, but still ..."

John pictured scopes and forceps, bits of larynx sandwiched between cover slips. He cleared his throat. "It's never too late to quit, I guess."

"Wise words, young man. Just because something's broken doesn't mean you keep on breaking it, am I right?"

"As rain, sir."

"Please, call me Obadiah," the old man said, tapping the nameplate with his cigarette.

Rock came back with the J&B and stuffed it in John's lap—a scotch-blend joey in the crotch of his jeans.

"So," the old man said. "What do you have for me?"

This was John's moment now. His alone to prove he belonged with the real world schemers—the ones outside his basement, the ones who live up to their namesakes and straddle desks like gods do. Because the real world is more than hoping and hatching plans. It's execution. It's sitting down and looking the man in the eye and making him flinch first, give up the goods. Or at least a prevailing wage, some bennies maybe.

John looked the man in the eye. "The first thing you should know is I'm a man of rules. Lots of them. I believe a man is only a man who lives by certain rules, parameters and whatnot. The second thing is I do not believe in résumés; that's one of the rules. I cannot stress that enough. But in the interest of full disclosure I should tell you, my résumé, if I were to have one, would appear a tad spartan. You see, I'm a family man. I don't have any kids, per se, but I do have a mother, an ailing one. I take care of her. I take care of the bills, too, and the doctor's appointments, the medications. I believe family should always come first; my father taught me that. Another rule. He taught me a lot of things, my father. He was a blue-collar guy, a union man, real salt of the earth, worked with his hands, tools."

The old man cocked his head some. Rock leaned back on the wall, crossed his arms, glared.

John cleared his throat. "What I'm getting at, Obadiah ..."

"Sir," said Rock.

"Umm, yeah. I mean, what I'm getting at, sir, is what I lack in actual job-market experience I make up for in real-world experience. I'd be a valuable addition to the staff." John unbuttoned his collar then buttoned it again and, trying to muster up some Kelly courage, said, "I never flinch, sir."

The old man leaned back in his chair. Rock flexed his wifebeater tan and exhaled through his nose. John could feel the wobble bass through the hardwood, wished he could ride the sound and bodywave himself back to his small world, his mother, her basement. He stared at the spot in between the old man's eyes. The old man finally spoke.

"I am confused," he said, turning toward Rock. "Rock, are you confused?"

"Very confused," Rock said.

"Unconfuse me."

Rock slapped the darkness into John. "Cut the shit!" he said and slapped him back to light.

The old man blew vapor and watched Rock slap John out of his chair, rip the collar off his shirt.

"Where's Kelly, John?" said Rock. "Have you seen Kelly, John?"

John saw stars. "I don't understand ..."

"Neither do we, John," Rock said. "Kelly owes us money, John. Kelly said he'd pay us, John. Kelly said he's sending John with the money, John. Where's the goddamn money, John?"

Rock punctuated his words with his hands. He took John by the ears and thumbed the lobes until the cartilage broke and through him cackled blood and pain. He forced him to his feet, held him by the hair to keep him standing. He looked at the old man who looked back and said, "Well?"

Rock stuffed his hand in John's pants, cupped his balls, ripped the pockets off his khakis.

"Well?" the old man said. "What?"

"Not even a wallet, just some scale." Rock held the baggy up, tongued it.

"Ours?" the old man said. "Jesus Christ, Rock." He came from around his desk. "We don't care what you do with it as long as you pay for it. Don't they know that, Rock?"

"They don't even know," Rock said and put a knee in John's stomach. Dropped him.

"Please," John said. "Pleaseplease."

The old man leaned in and said, "Please?"

"Please," John said.

"My god, man. Where do you think you are?" the old man said. "Don't you know why you are here?"

"I only came for the pimp job," said John, his lip busting blood.

Rock leaned in, busted some more.

When John woke up he was back in his basement, shirtless and not alone. January in poom-poom shorts and a scoop-neck sweater. She brought ice, held it on his puffing mouse, his cauliflower ears. "At least he didn't close his hand," she said.

"He's a real teddy," said John.

"They actually make you look tough."

"Yeah?"

"Tough is always good." She switched hands. Dripping water traced her forearm.

"How'd I get home?"

"Checkered cab," January said. "Tipped extra cuz of the blood."

"And my mom?"

"She's up there. I was going to make something up about your shirt but I don't think she noticed anyway."

January and John sat in silence for a while. And then they didn't.

"Kelly's sorry, you know."

"Yeah?" said John.

"I don't know," she said. "Probably."

She dropped the bag in his lap and shook water from her hands. She pulled a wad of bills from the nest of adipose tissue, due south, and peeled off a crispy few. "For the cable," she said. "She's staring at snow up there."

John followed her red calves up the stairs, her fingertips on the banister. He heard the front door close and static from the television. He got up and palmed the money, squeezed it.

In the kitchen he warmed his mother's dinner—black bean patty and broccoli, something she'd have appreciated back when she remembered to appreciate things—he knuckled digits, prompted the whir and the yellow light. He leaned his crotch in toward the microwave and imagined the next scheme he hatched to be a sightless, wailing thing. Its primordial ooze made mordial through electromagnetic waves, dielectric heating. He'd leash it, drag it around the important places: Yellowstone, Stonehenge, all the stones. Even the corner where he copped stones. He'd hoist its dwarfined body onto his shoulder, sing praises into its soundless Tiny Tim ears.

"I have hopes for you," he'd say.

High ones.

The microwave dinged and his mother came salivating, dragging her walker with the tennis ball feet. John imagined another life in which her entrance would've been accompanied by studio applause, canned laughter, an obligatory nod to Pavlov. A world where a sandy-blond, *Tiger Beat* cupid would play his son, spit out wisdoms too wise for his age. John would trade barbs with him until he was too old to trade anything, his son old enough to hatch his own schemes, pilfer his own Social Security checks. He would let him shoulder the world for a while. Inherit a rule or two.

ACKNOWLEDGEMENTS

Thank you to J. K. Fowler and Nomadic Press for publishing this work; Isobel O'Hare for her wonderful edits; my writing mother, Jacqueline Doyle; Steve Gutierrez, friend and mentor; my originals, TJ Puckett and Sean McFarland; editors James Claffey, Kevin O'Cuinn, Maxine Vande Vaarst, Katherine Morrison, and Jason Cook; Kara Vernor for her kind words and support; and Ruth Madievski, thank you for the inspiration.

Heartfelt thanks to the journals where these stories first appeared: *Literary Orphans*: "Sometimes Pop is Inside of the Bottle; Sometimes the Bottle is Inside of Pop"; *Ampersand Review*: "Rats, Tricks, Legumes"; *Word Riot*: "Valentine Springs"; *Buffalo Almanack*: "Rules of the Game"

DANIEL RIDDLE RODRIGUEZ'S real name is Daniel Riddle Rodriguez. He is a full-time student and father from San Lorenzo, California, where he lives with his son. He is the author of *Low Village* (CutBank, 2016), and his publications include *Prairie Schooner, Fourteen Hills, Word Riot, Gulf Stream Magazine*, and others. He is thrilled to be here.